The Princess
and the
Dragon

by Lynne Benton

Illustrated by Beatrice Bencivenni

W
FRANKLIN WATTS
LONDON•SYDNEY

Notes on the series

TIDDLERS are structured to provide support for children who are starting to read on their own. The stories may also be used for sharing with children.

Starting to read alone can be daunting. **TIDDLERS** help by listing the words in the book for a check before reading, and by providing visual support and repeating words and phrases. These books will both develop confidence and encourage reading and rereading for pleasure.

If you are reading this book with a child, here are a few suggestions:

1. Make reading fun! Choose a time to read when you and the child are relaxed and have time to share the story.
2. Talk about the story before you start reading. Look at the cover and the blurb. What might the story be about? Why might the child like it?
3. Look also at the list of words below - can the child tackle most of the words?
4. Encourage the child to retell the story, using the jumbled picture puzzle.
5. Give praise! Remember that small mistakes need not always be corrected.

Here is a list of the words in this story.

Common words:

a	her	so
after	I	the
away	is	there
best	looked	was
came	my	went
cried	no	will
day	one	you
dragon	once	
he	shouted	

Other words:

friend	prince	save
happy	princess	

Once there was
a princess.

Her best friend
was a dragon.

The dragon looked
after her.

One day a prince came.

"No!" cried the princess.

"The dragon is my friend."

The prince went away.

The princess
was happy.

So was the dragon.

Puzzle Time

Can you find these
pictures in the story?

Which pages are the pictures from?

Turn over for answers!

Answers

The pictures come
from these pages:

a. pages 10–11

b. pages 6–7

c. pages 16–17

d. pages 4–5

First published in 2014 by
Franklin Watts
338 Euston Road
London
NW1 3BH

Franklin Watts Australia
Level 17/207 Kent Street
Sydney
NSW 2000

Text © Lynne Benton 2014
Illustration © Beatrice Bencivenni 2014
The rights of Lynne Benton to be
identified as the author and Beatrice
Bencivenni as the illustrator of this Work
have been asserted in accordance with the
Copyright, Designs and Patents Act, 1988.

A CIP catalogue record for this book is
available from the British Library.

ISBN 978 1 4451 3257 0 (hbk)
ISBN 978 1 4451 3260 0 (pbk)
ISBN 978 1 4451 3258 7 (ebook)
ISBN 978 1 4451 3259 4 (library ebook)

Series Editor: Jackie Hamley
Editor: Melanie Palmer
Series Advisor: Catherine Glavina
Series Designer: Peter Scoulding

Printed in China

Franklin Watts is a division of Hachette Children's Books,
an Hachette UK company. www.hachette.co.uk